Author's Acknowledgements

My sincere thanks to the following people for their involvement in creating this book and cd:

Illustrations: Pegi Ballenger
Layout and design: Lisa Tarr

Editing:
Rabbi Jamie Arnold, Jean Bell, Irene Clurman,
Jesse Larner, Ken Larner, Carol Larner,
Deborah Stellini, Rachel White, Sarah White

CD Credits:
Songs sung by Daniel Stellini
Narrator's voice - Deborah Stellini
Rabbi's voice - Daniel Stellini
Mouse's voice - Nancy Larner

Text copyright © 2008 by Nancy Larner;
Illustration copyright © 2008 by Pegi Ballenger;
Design and Layout by Lisa Tarr, TarrArt LLC, www.tarrart.com;

Published in USA by Song Sparrow Press, Evergreen, CO.
Printed in Hong Kong.
ISBN Number: 978-0-9814654-0-1;
Library of Congress Control Number: 2007910362;
Price: $19.95 US

For additional information or to order more books,
email: nancylarner@songsparrowpress.com.

www.songsparrowpress.com or www.mouseandtherabbi.com

A Mouse in

the Rabbi's Study

by Nancy Larner
illustrations by Pegi Ballenger

Song Sparrow Press
Evergreen, Colorado

To Saguache County
Public Library,
Nancy Larner

Glossary

Bagel (BAY-g'l) - a hard doughnut-shaped roll

Blintzes (BLINTZ-es) - a thin rolled pancake dough rolled with a filling of cream cheese or fruit

Challah (KHAH-leh) - a braided loaf of bread, glazed with egg white made especially for the Sabbath or special holidays

Hamantaschen (HO-men-ta-shin) - a triangular-shaped pastry representing Haman's hat, traditionally filled with poppy seed or fruit

Hanukkah (KHON-eh-keh) - an eight-day Jewish holiday, also known as the "Festival of Lights." It commemorates the victory of Judah and the Maccabees in their fight for religious freedom and the re-dedication of the Temple of Jerusalem.

Kugel (KIGL) - a pudding of noodles or potatoes

Latkes (LOT-kehs) - a potato pancake fried in oil

L'Shannah Tova (l-shana-TOVA) - Happy New Year

Maccabee (MA-ke-bee) - a Hebrew word meaning "hammer." Judah Maccabee, the leader of a revolt against the Syrian-Greeks, was known for his great strength.

Mandelbrot (MAN-d'l-brot) - a hard cookie, similar to biscotti

Matzoh (MOTT-seh) - an unleavened bread eaten during Passover

Mazel (MA-z'l) - luck

Menorah (men-AW-ra) - the nine-branched candelabrum lit on Hanukkah.

Oneg (O-neg) - a Hebrew word meaning "delight." It generally means a time for refreshments after Friday Shabbat services.

Rabbi (RA-bye) - teacher

Passover (PAS-over) - the week-long holiday commemorating the Jews' deliverance from enslavement in Egypt

Purim (POOR-im) - a festival celebrating the rescue of the Jews by Queen Esther from Haman's plot to exterminate them.

Rosh Hashanah (rawsh-ha-SHAW-neh) - the new year, at which time forgiveness is asked. Apples and honey are traditionally eaten in the hope of a sweet new year ahead.

Shabbat (sha-BOT) - Sabbath, which, for Jews, begins each Friday at sundown and ending Saturday at sundown, when three stars appear in the sky. It separates the work week from a time of relaxation and reflection.

Shamas (SHAH-mes) - the candle that stands taller than, and lights, the other eight candles on the menorah

Sukkah (SUK-kah) - a temporary booth or hut built outdoors with only three walls and a roof made of branches. It is traditionally decorated with fruit and flowers.

Sukkot (suk-KOT) - the Festival of Booths, held at harvest time.

Synagogue (SIN-a-gog) - the house of worship for Jews

Yom Kippur (yom-kip-POOR) - the most important holiday of Jewish people, who fast and pray, asking God for forgiveness.

For Mom,
who taught me to love the
holidays through her cooking
of these delicious foods.
-NL

To my husband and our family,
Thank you for all your love
and encouragement.
-PB

No one knew how they got in, but Mrs. Golder shrieked and held up the evidence.
"What's wrong?" asked Mrs. Cohen, alarmed as she ran into the synagogue
kitchen and saw the panic on Mrs. Golder's face.
"They've bitten the fringe off the new tea towels, and look here!
There's a hole on the bottom of this cracker box."

"Mice! Mice!" they both shrieked and ran into the secretary's office. "Call the exterminator! Buy a mouse trap! Plug up the holes!"

The secretary got busy on the phone trying to find help. Then Mrs. Golder canceled the ladies luncheon that was to be held that very day in the social hall and left.

About 9:00 that morning Rabbi Saltzman bumbled into his office. He was a roundish man who often forgot something like tucking in his shirt tails or wiping from his beard a few stray crumbs left over from his last meal. But the twinkle in his kind eyes made you forget his personal oversights.

The rabbi was planning to sit down quietly at his desk with a cup of tea and some of Mrs. Saltzman's freshly baked *mandelbrot*, and write the sermon for the upcoming *Shabbat* service.

He no sooner set his briefcase on his desk when he noticed out of the corner of his eye something scurrying across its surface. Thinking it was just his imagination,
he shrugged his shoulders, went into the kitchen, and made himself some tea.
Setting his cup on his desk, he opened the foil package of mandelbrot, dunked the hard crisp cookie into his tea, leaned back in his chair, and thought about the sermon.

"Now let's see," he said, stroking his beard, "what does our congregation need to learn this week?"

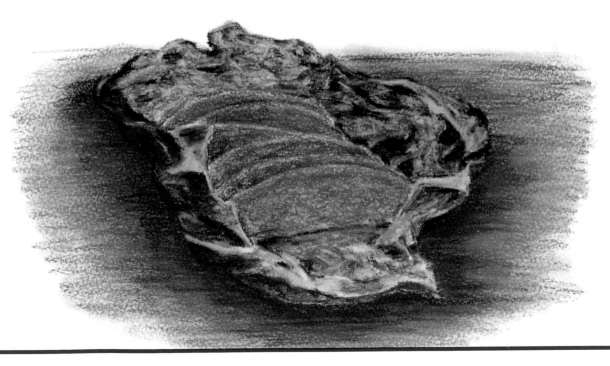

If you haven't already guessed, Rabbi Saltzman loved to eat. After a few more dunks and a few more sips of tea, an idea popped into the rabbi's head.

"Nothing like a good cup of tea to get the mind working. That's what I always say."

He opened his desk drawer, removed a large writing pad, and was reaching for a pencil when there, peering around the side of the pencil can, was a little, gray, trembling mouse with jet black eyes and white tips on his ears.

"Now what have we here?" asked the rabbi kindly.

"Excuse me, sir, but it's getting very cold in the evenings now, and my mother and father and all of my brothers and sisters, aunts, uncles, and cousins would like to find a place to stay for the winter. We like your kitchen. It's nice and warm, and there's plenty to eat."

"Then what are you doing in my study?" the rabbi asked.

"Well, sir, I went exploring a little too far from my family, but I did find some yummy crusts and cookie crumbs on the floor in here."

The rabbi laughed. "I do make a bit of a mess when I eat." Then he got an idea.

"Let's make a bargain. I'll let you stay here for the winter if you help me keep my study tidy by eating all the crumbs I drop……. but you'll have to stay out of sight when I have guests."

The little mouse's eyes grew large with excitement.

"As for your family, they can't stay here. Perhaps they would like the shed where we keep the lawn mower. There is enough grass seed to last the winter."

The rabbi pointed out the window to a small shed at the far edge of the property. "With the cold weather coming, the janitor won't need to cut the grass until spring. While you're staying with me, I will tell you many Jewish stories you can share with your family later."

"It's a deal," said the mouse ecstatically, and the rabbi shook the mouse's paw.
"By the way, what's your name?" asked the rabbi.
"Well sir, my parents call me Number 34."
The rabbi looked at him a little sadly.

"Since you will be part of our congrega-tion for the winter, how would you like a proper Hebrew name? I will call you *Mazel*, which means luck. We have both had good luck today!"

"Yes!" The mouse smiled. He liked his new name.

With that the rabbi began teaching Mazel the meaning of *Shabbat*.

"On the seventh day of creation God rested, so Jewish people follow God's commandment and stop their busy schedules at sundown on Friday night. We light the Sabbath candles, bless the children, drink wine, and eat *challah*, followed by a delicious meal. After that we sing Shabbat songs, and some families go to the synagogue to pray.

This is the time a family spends reading, studying, and simply being together. The most important thing is that Shabbat is a separation from the rest of the week, a time for relaxation. When three stars appear in the night sky on Saturday, Shabbat is over."

After services that Friday night, refreshments were served at the *oneg*. There was a crowd around the rabbi congratulating him on his thoughtful sermon, entitled "Showing Kindness to Large and Small Alike."

Before he left for home that night, the rabbi unlocked his study and left a small piece of challah for Mazel on a plate in the corner.

By September's end, Mazel's head was filled with wonderful stories.
At *Rosh Hashanah*, Mazel learned about changing some of his behaviors to make himself a better mouse.

"*L'Shannah Tova*, Happy New Year," the rabbi said to Mazel, and he laid a plate of apple cores and luscious drips of honey on his desk after services.

On *Yom Kippur*, Mazel felt very hungry. "Why do I have to wait to eat when I'm so hungry now?" Mazel inquired.

"It's the holiest day of the year," explained the rabbi. "Today we stop everything, even eating, in order to talk to God and ask forgiveness for any wrongdoing. You'll feel better at break-the-fast."

At last, long shadows appeared on the browning lawn. It was sundown. After an entire day of praying and fasting, everyone was hungry.

The whole congregation gathered in the social hall. Mrs. Golder brought her famous *kugel,* and Mrs. Cohen smiled proudly when everyone oooood and aaaaahed over the platters of *blintzes* she prepared. There were also egg and tuna salads, pickled herring, onion *bagels*, and a mountain of sweets.

The rabbi ate heartily. It had been a long, meaningful day of fasting and prayer, and his stomach was growling. He filled his plate with a second helping, then remembered he had some reading to finish in his study. The rabbi set the plate on his desk.

He read for hours and, while he read, he ate absentmindedly. Mazel sat under the desk chair and gobbled up an avalanche of noodle kugel bits and cheese from the blintzes. Pieces of hard-boiled egg rolled off the rabbi's lap onto the floor. Mazel never tasted anything so delicious -- and for dessert, sweet spongecake crumbs. By the time the rabbi turned off the light and locked the study door behind him, Mazel had fallen asleep with a very full tummy. The long day of fasting was worth the wait.

One October morning the rabbi announced it was time to learn about *Sukkot*, and about harvesting and building a little hut called a *sukkah*.

"That's what my family does also," Mazel said excitedly. "We gather food for the winter and bring it to a nice warm nest."

The rabbi smiled when he gave it some thought. "It's almost the same," he said.

"Jews hang fruits and vegetables in the sukkah, which is a temporary structure.

You must be able to see the stars through the roof. We eat in the sukkah and invite friends to join us for meals. Sometimes we sleep there as well."

"That's what we do too, eat and sleep in our nest!" proclaimed Mazel.

And so the rabbi continued telling Mazel stories throughout the winter. At *Hanukkah* time, Mazel felt like a courageous *Maccabee* fighting for the right to worship as a Jew.

He especially liked seeing the eight *menorah* candles, with the *shamas* towering above the others.

The rabbi told him the story of the destruction of the temple and about the small container of oil the Jews found that burned for eight days. That allowed enough time for them to clean the temple so that they could worship there again.

But the smell of latkes frying in oil in the synagogue kitchen at the children's Hanukkah party nearly drove him wild.

He could barely restrain himself from making an appearance in the kitchen to get a taste, but remembered his bargain with the rabbi and waited until he heard the key in the lock. He hoped the rabbi had some latkes for him and, of course, he did. Mazel tried them first with applesauce, then with sour cream.
But his favorite was just plain latkes.

In March the rabbi told Mazel the amazing story of *Purim*.

"Brave Queen Esther, with the help of her cousin Mordecai, persuaded her king that Haman was planning to do away with all the Jews in the kingdom. She exposed Haman's plan, and, instead of the Jews, Haman was sent to the gallows."

Oh how Mazel hated that Haman. He stamped his little mouse foot every time Haman's name was mentioned.

As much as he loved the Purim story, he loved *hamantaschen* even more. The rabbi poured over his books until long after the Purim carnival was over and the synagogue was quiet once again.

He must have had a difficult passage to understand because large pieces of delicious hamantaschen fell onto his beard and down into his lap, bounced off, and fell to the floor between loud slurps of hot tea.
It simply rained hamantaschen crumbs, and Mazel was quite busy tidying up long after the rabbi left for the night.

Frogs

Locusts

Darkness

Wild Beasts

Hail

The weather was growing warmer. There was no longer a chill
in the air and Mazel, knowing what this meant, felt sad.
Soon he would have to leave the rabbi and the synagogue.
The rabbi noticed Mazel looking a little glum.
"Don't be sad my friend, I have a marvelous story to tell you,"
smiled the rabbi, and he began telling Mazel the most exciting
story he ever heard.

"The Jews were slaves in Egypt," he began. "God spoke to
Moses from a burning bush and chose him to lead the Jews
out of Egypt to freedom. God helped Moses bring ten awful
plagues to convince Pharaoh, the king of Egypt, to let the
Jews go.   During each plague Pharaoh promised to let the
Jews go free, but afterwards he changed his mind."

River turns to
blood

Boils

Gnats

Cattle died

After the tenth plague, Mazel sighed with relief when first-born sons in Jewish families were saved from the angel of death as it passed over their homes.

"That is why we call this the *Passover* story," explained the rabbi.

"Moses told the Jews to gather their belongings quickly, and he led them to the Red Sea. In front of them lay the sea and behind them the Pharaoh's army was fast approaching. The Jewish people were very frightened."

"How could they escape?" asked Mazel, his eyes growing as big as saucers. Then the rabbi told the most exciting part of all.

"At that moment, God made the waters of the sea part, and the Jews walked safely to the other side. Then the water closed on the Pharaoh's army and all the soldiers were drowned."

"Then what happened?"

"Well," continued the rabbi, "the Jews wandered through the desert for forty years. During this time God gave Moses the Ten Commandments, which are very important rules we still live by today."

"Wow" exclaimed Mazel, "Moses was some important guy."

"He certainly was," the rabbi said with a laugh.
"Tell me rabbi. What special food is eaten for Passover?"

"Something delicious that you will be happy to know makes lots of crumbs! Remember when the Jews had to leave their homes quickly?"
Mazel nodded.

"Well they didn't have time to let their bread rise. The result was flat bread which we call *matzah*. That's the special food for the holiday, the bread of freedom."

With that the rabbi pulled a large cracker from the box on his desk, broke off a piece and bit into it. Crumbs flew everywhere -- on the rabbi's beard, on his lap, his desk, and all over the floor. Mazel scurried to clean up the crumbs.

"Delicious!" they exclaimed in unison, and the rabbi took another bite.

Mazel ate his fill of matzah that night, but he didn't sleep well because he knew his time for leaving was coming soon.

In the morning the rabbi reminded Mazel the grass was starting to turn green and, after a few more rainy nights, the janitor would be opening up the shed where the lawn mower is stored and where Mazel's family spent the winter. Mazel knew it was time to say good-bye.

"We made a good bargain, Mazel, my friend, and now you must go back to your family. They have missed you, and you will have much to share with them."

"Who will keep your study tidy?" asked Mazel sadly.

The rabbi opened the closet door and there stood a brand new electric vacuum cleaner.

"Oh," said Mazel looking down at his feet trying desperately to hold back the mouse tears stinging in his eyes. The rabbi's face became very serious.

"Mazel, our bargain was much more than a tidy study and a place to stay for the winter. We became good friends. I looked forward to sharing stories with you each day, and I will miss your company."

"And I looked forward to seeing you each day too, rabbi," said Mazel wiping away his tears. "I learned so much that I can now tell my family."

"We will part with great gifts in our hearts," said the rabbi warmly. "We are both blessed."

With that the rabbi shook Mazel's paw and, as quickly as you can say "hamantaschen," Mazel disappeared through a hole in the wall and was outside. He raced through the tall, green grass making his way to the far end of the property and the shed where his family spent the winter. He had missed them more than he realized and was looking forward with great anticipation to seeing his mother, father, sisters, brothers, aunts, and uncles. He wondered how many new cousins he must have by now.

He couldn't wait to tell them about the Maccabees, brave Queen Esther, the ten plagues, and much, much more that the wonderful Rabbi Saltzman had taught him.

Within a few days the janitor unlocked the shed door for the first spring mowing.

When he looked inside, he could hardly believe his eyes.